This book belongs to:

....

....

Editor: Carly Madden
Designer: Rachel Lawston
Editorial Director: Victoria Garrard
Art Director: Laura Roberts-Jensen

First published in the UK in 2015 by QED Publishing
A Quarto Group company, The Old Brewery, 6 Blundell Street, London, N7 9BH

www.qed-publishing.co.uk

A catalogue record for this book is available from the British Library.

ISBN 978 1 78493 089 9

Printed in China

FiNS, FLUFF and OTHER STUFF

By Bruno Merz and Dreda Blow
Illustrated by Bruno Merz

QED Publishing

If I were made of **scales** and **fins**,
with tangled seaweed hair,

I'd have to leave my fishy friends to swim back **up for air.**

If I were made of **fluffy** stuff,
I'd quickly have enough,
of hearing names like Snuggle Boo
and Pookie Wookie **Puff.**

If I were made of **soapy** suds
and **clean** right to my core...

...I'd leave a slippery **bubble** trail
behind me on the **floor.**

If I were made of **water**
in a bathtub or a jug,

I'd hope no one
would drink me or **someday pull the plug!**

If I were made of **lollipops**,
liquorice swirls and **sweets**...

...I'd slowly lose my **sugary** limbs to everyone I **meet!**

If I were made of **cobwebs,**
on the ceiling I could play.
But my silky strings would capture

creepy-crawlies on the **way!**

If I were made of **needles,**
like a **cactus,** oh so tall,

I'd make a **great goalkeeper,**
but **POP** a lot of **balls!**

If I were made of **flowers,**
I'd befriend the **buzzing bees...**

...but **pollen** from my fragrant **blooms** would **cause** the world to **sneeze!**

If I were made of **twigs** and **leaves**, the birds would build their **nests** among my **mossy** branches...

...but **I'd never get a rest!**

If I were made of **feathers**,
although I'd **try** and **try**,

I'd **run** and **jump** and
flap my **arms**,

but have **no wings to fly.**

If I were made of **metal**, staying **dry** would be a **must.**

My friends could **splash** in **puddles** but in the **rain** I'd **rust!**

If I were made of **skin** and **bones**,
with **freckles** on my nose...

Hey wait, that sounds familiar,
that's **ME** down to my **toes!**

I can **somersault** and **cartwheel**

or **dance** the **jitterbug.**

I can build a **pillow igloo,**

or give my **dog** a **hug.**

I can run so **fast** my legs **blur** or **hide** under my **bed.**

I can **sing** a **silly melody**

while **standing on my head.**

So after thinking **very** carefully
of **all** that I could be...

Yippee! I'm really quite **content** and **lucky** to be **ME!**

Next Steps

Show the children the cover. Can they guess what the story is about from looking at the cover?

In the story, the boy thinks of many different things he could be made of. Ask the children which materials they think sound like the most fun and which ones might be uncomfortable.

Can the children think of other things they could be made of?

Ask the children to draw pictures of themselves made of their favourite things.

There are lots of rhyming words in the book, like 'fluff' and 'stuff'. Ask the children to think of as many words as they can to rhyme with the following: bunny, hat, snake, rose, tree.

Discuss the story with the children and think about how our bodies work. Ask the children to think of things that we can do as humans that animals may not be able to.

There are lots of different animals in the book. Ask the children to look through the book again and see how many animals they can spot.